W9-CFH-036

Sink or Swim

Story by Valerie Coulman
Pictures by Rogé

Lobster Press™

Coulman, Valerie, 1969-
Sink or Swim
Text © 2003 Valerie Coulman
Illustrations © 2003 Rogé Girard

Published by
Lobster Press™
1620 Sherbrooke Street West, Suites C & D
Montréal, Québec   H3H 1C9
Tel. (514) 904-1100 • Fax (514) 904-1101
www.lobsterpress.com

Publisher & Editor: Alison Fripp

Graphic Design & Production: Tammy Desnoyers

Distributed in the United States by:
Publishers Group West
1700 Fourth Street
Berkeley, CA 94710

Distributed in Canada by:
Raincoast Books
9050 Shaughnessey Street
Vancouver, BC V6P 6E5

We acknowledge the financial support of the Government
of Canada through the Book Publishing Industry
Development Program (BPIDP) for our publishing activities.

The Canada Council | Le Conseil des Arts
for the Arts | du Canada

We acknowledge the support of
the Canada Council for the Arts
for our publishing program.

National Library of Canada Cataloguing in Publication

Coulman, Valerie, 1969-
        Sink or swim / Valerie Coulman ; illustrated by Rogé Girard.

ISBN 1-894222-54-7

        I. Rogé, 1972- II. Title.

PS8555.O82295S55 2003   jC813'.6   C2003-902654-X
PZ7

Printed and bound in Hong Kong.

"It sure is hot today!" Morris complained to Ralph as they rested under a shady tree. "We need to find a way to cool off."

Ralph was watching a duck family splash
in the pond on the far side of the meadow.
"We could go swimming," he said.

Morris turned to stare.

"Ralph, we don't know how to swim."

"Well, not yet, we don't," Ralph assured him.
"But we could learn."

"Come on," Ralph jumped to his feet.
"We need to find someone to teach us how to swim."

At the pond, Ralph said hello to the
duck family he had been watching earlier.

"Would you teach me and my friend to swim?" he asked.

One of the ducklings quacked,

"Cows can't
swim!"

And the little ducks started laughing so hard that
they rolled over and got water up their noses.

Ralph laughed too. "Well, not yet, they don't.
But maybe you could help us learn."

As the ducklings coughed and spluttered, their mother explained, "We swim by resting on the water on our bellies and kicking our feet under us. It's really very easy."

Ralph thought that did sound easy, so he
tried to rest on the water like a duck.

He sank like a stone.

When he came up, he was spluttering
as much as the baby ducks.
"See!" Morris called from the shore.
"I don't think cows were meant to swim."
"I think it takes practice." Ralph sneezed.

"And I think I need something to
keep the water out of my nose."
He blinked and added, "and my eyes."

Ralph went into the swim shop on Main Street.
"I'm learning to swim but I need something to
keep the water out of my eyes and my nose."
Bob, the owner, looked surprised.
"I've never had a cow ask for nose
plugs or goggles before . . . probably
because cows don't swim."

"Not yet, they don't," Ralph smiled.
"But I'm learning."

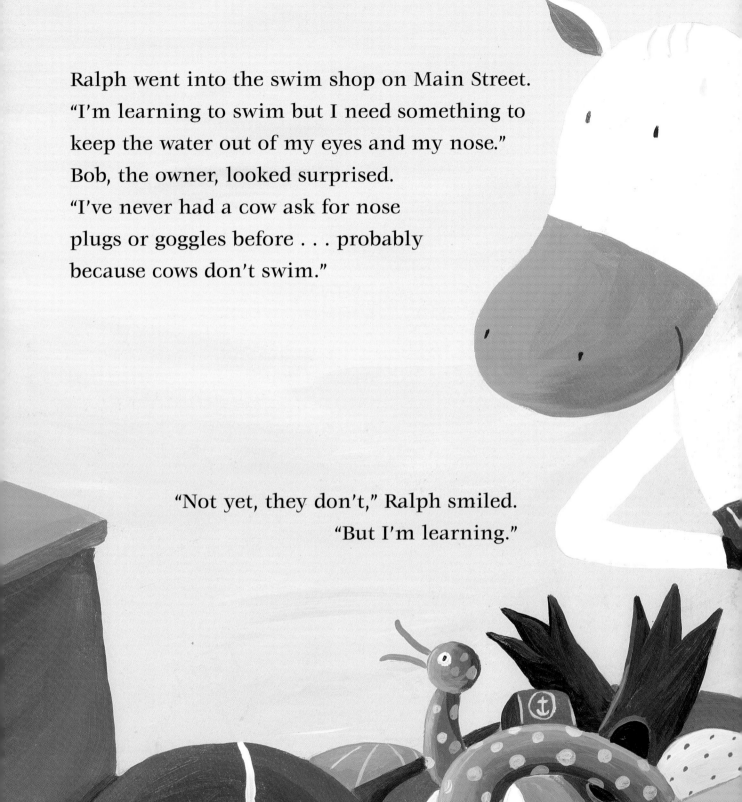

"Well," Bob looked around. "Try these."

Soon Ralph was back at the pond and ready to try again.

This time he asked a turtle that was floating nearby.
"Excuse me, but could you teach me how to swim?"

The turtle opened one eye, then opened both
eyes to stare at Ralph. "Cows don't swim."
"Not yet, they don't," Ralph said.
"But I'm going to try. How do you swim?"

The turtle lifted one flipper out of the water. "I use these. They help push me through the water when I swim. But you don't have flippers. You have hooves." And the turtle dove down into the cool water and swam away. "He's right, Ralph," said Morris.

Back at Bubbles Bob's Swim Shop, Bob sold Ralph the biggest flippers he had. "You'll probably want two pairs."

Morris had waited at the pond.

"Maybe that frog could tell us how he swims."

So Ralph asked the frog.

"I use my legs to push through the water. But when I want to relax, I just float on a lily pad or a log. It holds me up."

"Float?" Ralph thought out loud.
"If I could float, that would
help me swim, wouldn't it?"

He tried over . . .

and over . . .

and over.

Bob looked up as Ralph came into the shop.
"Can you swim yet?"

"Not yet. I need something to help me float.
The frog uses a lily pad but it was too small for me.
And the log kept rolling
over when I tried
to sit on it."
Ralph shook
water from one
ear as he remembered.

"Hmmm . . ." Bob looked around the store.
"I think this should work." And he brought down a big
surfboard. "This should hold you up without rolling over."

By the end of the afternoon, Ralph was able to
float on his surfboard and swim around the pond.
He was wonderfully cool, and was waiting for
Morris to return from the swim shop.

Morris returned to find Ralph staring at his surfboard. "How hard do you think it would be to stand on it?" "Oh, no, Ralph!" Morris exclaimed. "Cows may be able to float and swim but they definitely do not surf!"

Ralph grinned.

"Not yet they don't."

The end